WARRENER

A Picnic for Bunnykins

Illustrated by

Walter Hayward

Viking Kestrel

ALSO BY WARRENER

Two Bunnykins out to Tea

VIKING KESTREL

Penguin Books Ltd, Harmondsworth, Middlesex, England
Viking Penguin Inc., 40 West 23rd Street, New York, New York 10010, U.S.A.
Penguin Books Australia Ltd, Ringwood, Victoria, Australia
Penguin Books Canada Ltd, 2801 John Street, Markham, Ontario, Canada L3R 1B4
Penguin Books (N.Z.) Ltd, 182-190 Wairau Road, Auckland 10, New Zealand

First published in 1984

ISBN 0-670-80052-X

Library of Congress catalog card number: 83-23532
(British Library Cataloguing in Publication Data available)

Printed in Great Britain

The rabbit characters from which the now traditional
Bunnykins ® image evolved were created by an English
nun. Royal Doulton discovered her pencil drawings
in the 1930s and transformed them into the colourful
tableware and figures that have delighted
generations of children ever since.

Royal Doulton's own artists have continued the theme
and today designer Walter Hayward is responsible for
creating new scenes, each telling its own story with
an ageless charm and artistry, for use on their range
of gift pottery cherished by children the world over.

Once upon a bunnytime,
when the sun shone bright
on a little house called The Warren,
Mr Bunnykins said to his family:
'What about a picnic
in the high hills today?'

Then all the little Bunnykins
jumped for joy and clapped their paws
and shouted: 'Hurrah! Hurrah! A picnic!'
    Mrs Bunnykins said anxiously:
'But suppose it rains?
Suppose it hails?
Suppose it snows?
Suppose we all catch our deaths of cold?'
    Then Mr Bunnykins said:
'Don't fuss, my dear! I smell fine weather.'

Mrs Bunnykins knew
that she could trust
her husband's nose, so she said:
'What shall we take to eat on our picnic?'

One little bunny said: 'Peanuts!'
Another little bunny said: 'And popcorn!'
Another little bunny said: 'And pies!'
Another little bunny said:
'And peppermints!'
Another little bunny said: 'And peaches!'
Another little bunny said:
'And pink cupcakes!'

And the bunny who was littlest of all —
except for Baby Bunnykins — said:
'And gingerbread bunnies
with currant eyes!'
He always helped his mother
to make them,
and they were his favourite thing.
This little bunny's name was Bunting.

Mrs Bunnykins said:
'We'll take all those nice things;
and I have enough gingerbread bunnies

ready baked to take one each,
and an extra one, in case one breaks.
That can be so disappointing.

But we must take other bunny food
as well.
We must take lots of lettuces.'
'And ample apples,' said Mr Bunnykins.

'And a ration of radishes,' said Mrs
Bunnykins.
    'And a carrier-bag full of carrots,'
said Mr Bunnykins. 'I will carry it myself,
for safety.'
    'And what shall we take
to drink on our picnic?'
asked Mrs Bunnykins.

Mr Bunnykins said:
'We shan't need to take anything.
There will be springs of pure water
coming out from the high hillsides –
water so pure and clean
that we can safely drink it.'

'Then that's all right,' said Mrs
Bunnykins.

'Let's pack our food and be off!'
   They all helped to pack
the big picnic basket.
They put in the peanuts
and the popcorn and the pies
and the peppermints and the peaches
and the pink cupcakes,
as well as lots of lettuces
and ample apples and a ration of radishes

and, on top of everything else,
very carefully,
they packed the gingerbread bunnies
with currant eyes. The picnic basket was
so heavy that everyone
took turns at helping to carry it.

They set off. They walked
and they walked
and they walked,
until they reached the high hills.
Then they climbed
and they climbed
and they climbed.

All the time the sun shone,
and the Bunnykins family
began to feel very hot and very thirsty.

Suddenly Mr Bunnykins said:
'Look!'
And there was a spring of pure,
clean water gushing out of the hillside,
just as he had promised.
The water flowed away down the hillside
in a stream that grew wider
and wider as it went; but the water
was purest and cleanest –
and oh! so very cold –
where it began.

So that was where the bunnies drank.
They drank as much cold, clear water
as they wanted,
and no one was thirsty any more.
Then they sat down
to eat their picnic.
They ate fast, as bunnies do.

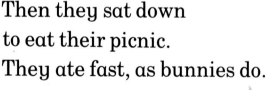

Before you could say 'Jack Rabbit!'
they had eaten up the peanuts
and the popcorn and the pies
and the peppermints and the peaches
and the pink cupcakes and the lettuces
and the apples and the radishes
and the carrots.

They ate their gingerbread bunnies
with currant eyes; and none of them
had been broken, after all,
so the extra one was left at the bottom
of the picnic basket.

After their picnic,
all the little bunnies played games.
They played Tig
and Blind Bunny's Buff
and Hide-and-Seek;
but, more than anything else,
they played Jump-across-the-Stream.
They jumped where the stream was widest.

Mr and Mrs Bunnykins dozed in the sun
and listened to their children
shouting and laughing. Suddenly they
heard
SPLASH!

And there was poor Bunting,
the littlest bunny, who had tried to jump
the stream where it was too wide for him,
and had fallen in.

The stream was not very deep,
and his family soon pulled Bunting out;
but oh! the water had been cold,
and Bunting was soaked
to the fur under his red jacket
and to the skin under his fur.

Mrs Bunnykins cried:
'Take your wet clothes off at once,
Bunting!'

Then she gave him
the last gingerbread bunny
to cheer him up, and it did a little,
because it was his favourite thing.

Then she told him: 'Now run, run, run
in the sun, my bun! Or you'll catch
your death of cold!'

So Bunting ran and ran and ran,
as only a bunny can,
in nothing but his brown fur
and his white tail.

He ran WILD.

When all his brothers and sisters saw him,

they wanted to do the same.

They stripped off their clothes

and ran in nothing but their brown fur

and their white tails.

They ran and ran and ran.

They ran WILD.

Mr Bunnykins said anxiously:
'Whatever will the neighbours think?'
  But Mrs Bunnykins said:
'Don't fuss, my dear!
There aren't any neighbours
in these high hills.
And bunnies will be bunnies, after all.'

Mr Bunnykins knew he could trust
his wife's judgement, so he just said:
'I'll spread out Bunting's wet clothes
in the sun to dry.'

Little Bunting ran and ran until his fur
and his tail were quite dry,
and he was dry right down to his skin.
While he ran, his brothers and sisters ran
with him,
just for the fun of it.

At last they all stopped running
and put their clothes on again.
Then, in a most proper manner,
the Bunnykins family went home
to The Warren,
to supper
and then to bed.
    And that is the end of this bunnytale.